Christmas with Billy and Me

Christmas with Billy and Me

A Short Story

BY GIOVANNA FLETCHER

MICHAEL JOSEPH
an imprint of
PENGUIN BOOKS

PENGUIN BOOKS

UK | USA | Canada | Ireland | Australia
India | New Zealand | South Africa

Penguin Books is part of the Penguin Random House group of companies
whose addresses can be found at global.penguinrandomhouse.com.

Penguin
Random House
UK

First published 2014

002

Text copyright © Giovanna Fletcher, 2014

The moral right of the author has been asserted

Set in 12/14 pt Garamond MT Std
Typeset by Jouve (UK), Milton Keynes
Printed in Great Britain by Clays Ltd, St Ives plc

A CIP catalogue record for this book is available from the British Library

ISBN: 978–0–718–18045–4

www.greenpenguin.co.uk

MIX
Paper from
responsible sources
FSC® C018179
www.fsc.org

Penguin Random House is committed to a
sustainable future for our business, our readers
and our planet. This book is made from Forest
Stewardship Council® certified paper.

To Santa, for spreading love and happiness far and wide.
It wouldn't be Christmas without your magical ways.
Keep up the good work.

Oh, and if I could have that kitchen extension I asked
for in my letter I'd be super grateful forevermore . . .;-)

If not, then an hour to myself in the bath with a glass of
wine would suffice. For now. As long as there's chocolate
available too . . . make them Ferrero Rocher! PLEASE!

I.

It won't surprise anyone to hear that one thing I hate about birthdays is having all the focus on me. I always feel uncomfortable at being soloed out and fussed over – it's embarrassing having people give me gifts, and I stupidly end up feeling selfish for hogging the limelight. Yes, I know that's what birthdays are about, and I love spoiling others on their special days, but when it comes to my own turn I tend to spend the entire time with a bright-red face as I cringe my way through it, longing for the day to end so that I can go back into my land of obscurity and blend seamlessly into the background.

But Christmas? Well, everyone is always in a joyously giving mood at Christmas, ready to sprinkle a little love wherever they can. It's a time when everyone gets to feel special and the attention is evenly divided as we all do our best to spread the festive cheer as far and wide as possible. We are happy to go out of our way to make anyone's day a little brighter, ready to give whatever it takes to raise a little smile from strangers and loved ones alike. How lovely!

Like many people, I'd say Christmas is my favourite time of the year. Plus, nowhere looks better than Rosefont Hill at Christmas. In the evenings the whole High

Street of our little village comes alive with festoon lighting hanging between each lamp post and a massive, beautifully decorated Christmas tree stands towards the bottom of the hill, on the green outside the church. The only thing that would make it look even more idyllic would be a white blanket of snow covering the ground. I've no doubt the local Women's Institute sit for hours pondering over how they can bring on the fluffy stuff – I can even imagine them doing some sort of weird snow dance in hope of its arrival, but a white Christmas is as rare as a hot English summer. When it does happen, though (just occasionally) the joy it brings with it is wonderful. Once it's driven through, of course, it turns into black mush and causes a few grumbles – it's ugly and icy then – but before that part comes the silence and beauty. It's breathtaking. Being on a hill means that we're pretty much brought to a standstill when it snows and I quite enjoy being cut off from the world for a little while as we sit cocooned in our little white, tranquil bubble until it leaves.

For me, the morning frost goes a long way to giving the illusion of snow, so I'm always thrilled on my early morning winter strolls to work. I love the arrival of a new season – each one bringing with it its own emotion: spring is full of hope; summer is freedom; autumn is a colourful release and winter brings an enchanting peace. It's hard to pick which one I enjoy the most– each time the new one arrives I remember its beauty and forget the previous one whose qualities have started to dim.

The first of December is always an important night of the calendar for folks of Rosefont Hill. Over the years a tradition has been created where the community gathers around the newly assembled tree – which would have been decorated to perfection by the aforementioned WI – to sing Christmas carols and 'ooh' and 'aah' as the lights get switched on and we're all struck by the wonderment a bit of electricity can bring. Sparkling magic! Then, once people start blowing into their hands declaring they are about to lose their fingers to frostbite, they walk up the hill to the teashop, where Molly and I are waiting (having snuck off ten minutes earlier) with warm hot chocolate and yummy mince pies for all to devour merrily.

This year is the first time I'm taking on that challenge without the magnificent Molly and, to be honest, it's only the havoc of getting everything ready that's pulling me through my first Molly-less Christmas – there's been so much to do. Six months have passed since the horrific day my best friend lost her cancer battle and handed me the reins of her beloved teashop. It hasn't been an easy task, but somehow I've managed to pull it off. So far.

Molly loved Christmas; she loved any occasion that meant she was surrounded by people she could care for and spoil – having lost her husband Albert long before I started working for her, and her only son having moved to Australia with his family –she relished company and making others smile. She'd do

3

anything to make someone's day just that little bit brighter. Which is why I want, more than anything, to make the night absolutely perfect so that, if she were looking down on me from her little cloud in heaven, she'd be proud.

In the lead-up to what will hopefully be a blissful evening ahead (if I manage to keep my anxiety at bay), I'm behind the counter at Molly's-on-the-Hill, covered in flour, edible glitter and a layer of unattractive sweat as I battle to get organized in time. My skinny black jeans stick to my legs more than usual and I wish I hadn't worn a long-sleeved top to work that morning – even if it is a festive grey number with a jolly snowman on the front. In fact, I wish I'd opted to be a naked chef for the day and pranced around in just my red polka-dotted apron and matching headscarf – I'd have been far cooler. There's still time, I jokily think as the thought of Miss Brown's face if I were to just abandon my clothes that very second causes a smile to creep up and momentarily remove the frown of concentration that's been plastered on my forehead all morning. Darn me and my prudish ways, I sigh, settling for being a stinking hot mess instead.

'Are you ready for tonight, love?' Mum asks as she pokes her head round the shop door, gliding her hand over her brown hair to make sure the wind hasn't caused it to blow out of control. She's never been one for mess.

'I think so.' I frown once more, looking around at

the mountains of cake, sausage rolls, mini cranberry-and-turkey pizzas and other Christmassy nibbles covering the counter top in front of me, all wrapped in clingfilm or under glass cake domes, waiting to be devoured by our guests later on. I'm particularly proud of my chocolate and hazelnut cannoli, they were a total experiment as I've never made anything like them before, but their crunchy shells look tantalizingly delicious.

We've done our best to make all the food look festive, too – either by winding holly and ivy around the serving plates, lightly sprinkling edible glitter over the top or, as I've done with the cheese platter, laying the yellow cubes out in the shape of a Christmas tree.

If the feast isn't enough to please everyone and get them into the jollifying spirit, then perhaps the beverages will. Gallons of mulled wine are currently being created on the stove by Billy. He's been an endless help in putting all the food together with me – he may not be the best cook in the world, but what he lacks in skill he makes up for in effort. He's always been keen to learn, ever since Molly taught him how to make scones for our first date, but tonight he's insisted on being in charge of the drinks.

Having dramatically declared he was taking a break from acting a few months before (he hadn't warned anyone before announcing it on one of the UK's biggest chat shows), he seems to enjoy taking on jobs around the shop whenever I let him. Which, I'll admit, isn't too often – after all, taking over Molly's has made me see that I'm capable of more than I ever realized. I'm not ready to lean on others too much now that I've finally found my feet and got into the swing of things. That being said, I'm not daft. I know there's no way I'd be able to get everything together without help from Billy and my nearest and dearest – thankfully they all offer repeatedly, and they don't seem to mind being bossed around by me – I might be seen as a timid character by some, but in certain situations I'm anything but a wallflower. I don't mind giving direction when it comes to the shop and making sure things are meticulously perfect. Although, saying that, everybody's always such good help that my feisty side stays locked away, but I know it's there, ready to reveal itself if ever it's needed – like the time a member of the paparazzi turned up on my doorstep on one of the worst days of my life and goaded me for a reaction. I'm ashamed to admit I ended up sticking my finger up at him. So unladylike, but SO necessary – even if it did mean I gave him what he wanted. It was just one of a handful of times that I've felt a fire flicker within me and cause a knee-jerk reaction – another was when I tipped an iced drink over a complete idiot of a guy when I worked in Coffee Matters in London. Needless to say, I'm overjoyed that life back in Rosefont Hill is as it was throughout my early childhood – peaceful and uneventful. Well . . . for the most part.

'She's been nibbling on her bottom lip all morning, Jane,' laughs Billy, chucking cinnamon sticks into his cauldron-like pot as he nudges my bum with his. 'And that frown of hers . . .' he cheekily whistles as his dark brown eyes widen in mock trepidation.

I roll my eyes in his direction, but can't help smiling at his gorgeous face as his eyes twinkle in his cheeky manner.

'Can I do anything?' Mum asks as she makes her way over to the counter and peers over it to see the progress we've made.

'To be honest, Mum, I think I'm nearly there.'

'Wonderful. Colin phoned earlier – he's still up for helping serve later.'

'Fantastic!'

Colin is a godsend! I wasn't too sure how I felt when Mum first told me she had a 'manfriend', but he's got such a heart of gold, it's impossible not to be pleased that Mum's found someone so kind and loving – a person to take care of her when I'm not around. And let's not forget how wonderful he's been to me. Not only did he play a huge part in the re-opening of the shop, but he also helped me express my grief over Molly's death in ways that I'll never forget or be able to thank him properly for.

Like most people, Colin comes with his own tales of sorrow. His wife died in her sleep a couple of years before he met my mum, leaving him alone with two children – Aaron, who's now ten years old and Charlotte, who's just eight.

Out of respect for Pauline, and so as not to confuse his young children prematurely, Colin waited

7

several months before introducing them to Mum, and then to me and Billy. Aaron is outgoing and loves sport. He's always either on his bike or has his skateboard with him, asking Billy to play with him whenever possible. Charlotte is the quieter one of the two and never goes anywhere without her Minnie Mouse cuddly toy – a companion she's had since birth. I've no doubt Minnie was once pristine and full of stuffing, but nowadays she's a little tattered from where she was clearly bitten and sucked by Charlotte during her teething years, and dragged everywhere since. It reminds me of my own childhood friend Mr Blobby, who I never left the house without.

I know the sadness that comes with losing a parent – I lost my own dad when I was eleven years old. For that reason alone I can't help but feel protective over Colin's young children. I've an innate desire to build new happy memories for them both, rather than have them longing sadly for the past and something that can never return or be replaced.

They're an adorable addition to our family – it's certainly a lot busier and warmer than when it was just me and Mum sharing a takeaway on a Friday night. Now it feels like a real family unit, even if it is a slightly mismatched one – but then, aren't most families like that these days?

With that in mind, this will be quite a special Christmas. It's the first one we'll be spending all together. More than previous years, I feel the darkness that usually surrounds that occasion has lifted. Instead, it's been replaced by hope. I want it to be as magical as possible.

'Anything you need me to do before I go home and get changed?' Mum asks.

'I don't think so . . .' I reply with a frown, looking down at our handiwork. 'Do you think this'll be enough?'

'Darling,' Mum replies with a chortle, ' I think there'll be enough for everyone to invite their extended families and still be able to take a doggy bag home. You'll be fine.'

'Are you sure?' I ask, before remembering that what's in front of us isn't even all of the food I've whipped together – there are other bits and pieces hidden away in the fridge and freezer, like the individual amaretto cheesecakes, my mozzarella and tomato sticks (decorated like mini snowmen with Christmas hats on) and my cranberry lemonade popsicles – I'm aware it's the wrong time of year for an icy treat, but I saw the recipe and fell in love with the idea of doing something a little different.

'Yes, there's mountains of food here – no one will go hungry, that's for sure. I'd be more worried about what he's putting into that pot.' Mum nods in Billy's direction.

I turn to see him chopping up some lemongrass, wrapping it into a cloth of spices and dropping it into his red wine.

'What?' he shrugs in reply to my raised eyebrows.

9

'It's going to be amazing. It's my own take on something I saw Gordon Ramsay do.'

'Are you experimenting?' I ask.

'No . . .' He sings while avoiding eye contact, focusing instead on picking bits of dried fruit from his festive T-shirt – which is a cartoon of Santa wearing a Christmas hat while holding a large glass of brandy, no doubt celebrating finishing his own seasonal chores. The top would look ridiculous on anyone else, but Billy has the ability to make anything look cool with his stylish quiff and the fact that he still looks every inch the effortless movie star.

'Billy?' I say, a little sterner.

'Maybe, but it'll be delicious, I swear.'

'Oh, Billy,' Mum laughs, covering her face with her hands and dramatically shaking her head. 'Lord help you if it's anything less than perfect.'

Billy looks so nervous that I let out a laugh. 'I'm sorry to say it, but she's right – the pressure's on. Although I'm sure it'll be lovely,' I smile, tugging at his arm and reaching up to plant a kiss on his reddening cheek.

'Thanks for the vote of confidence, ladies.'

'It'll be fine. I've never had a bad mulled wine in my life . . . though there's still time,' Mum teases, walking back towards the door. 'Right, I'm off. Give me a bell if you need anything.'

'Thanks, Mum,' I call as she waves and closes the door as she leaves.

'It's going to be great,' Billy says quietly with a pensive look on his face.

'I know,' I wink, grabbing his hand and kissing the back of it.

'Not the wine – well, that'll be great too, obviously,' he grins, pulling me closer and putting his arm around my waist. 'But I meant tonight. It's going to be fantastic.'

'I hope so.'

'Look how much effort you've put in! I've never seen a Christmas party with such heart poured into it. She'd have loved it, Sophie.'

'Thank you,' I smile, touched that he understands the importance of the night. It's not so much about the villagers or getting into the festive spirit, but more about my absent friend Molly and honouring what she loved.

'Although the mulled wine would definitely have been her favourite,' he winks, placing his hand under my chin to angle it towards him and kissing me on the mouth before I have a chance to argue.

2.

Much to the WI's disappointment, no snow fell as the community gathered around the village Christmas tree that evening. Instead, the air was crisp and the sky clear, allowing us to see the stars twinkling above as we sang 'O Little Town of Bethlehem', 'Away in a Manger' and 'Hark! The Herald Angels Sing' – to name just a few. Well-known songs that bring with them great joy when they're celebrated on a yearly basis. It makes my skin tingle to hear the village singing in chorus together – not that we're all particularly good singers or anything like that (I'm most definitely tone deaf), but because the unity of it is rather special and uplifting.

True to form, just before the last few songs were sung, Billy and I snuck off and made our way up to the shop to get the hot drinks ready. It was rather magical hearing the carols continuing as we held hands and walked up the empty village High Street. Looking at Billy with a smile and him kissing me in response, it was almost like having our own movie soundtrack guiding us to the festive party ahead.

Thanks to all our preparation we were standing in the shop window, looking down over the High Street, when the jolly crowd started making their way towards us. Hands were being rubbed together and coats were being wrapped a little tighter around bodies as they exhaled white streams of air into the night sky – everyone in much need of the warm delights awaiting them.

Hours later, and the shop's full of people – most of whom are wearing red Santa hats, festive jumpers (four of the men are even in identical red snowmen jumpers!) or bauble earrings, clearly dug out from wherever they've been hiding since last Christmas. No doubt they all have that musty smell of dust (mixed in with a slight touch of pine needles still lingering from the previous year's tree) that every decoration box gathers when it's not in use.

It's not just locals or those from nearby villages who've come along for the festivities – they've also brought along members of their extended families to join in the jovial evening. Everywhere I look there are people chatting away and laughing – it's lovely to see Molly's-on-the-Hill as a hub of such friendly activity.

I'm behind the counter washing glasses as Mrs Wallis tells me all about her grandson Russell – we went on a date years ago, and he's now married to a sweet woman called Hannah and has twin boys. She always likes to keep me in the loop, but on this occasion there's no need as I spotted them all earlier in the evening walking into the shop. That's something else I love about Christmas – all year long I hear from elderly customers about their families and grandchildren (for years it was only grandsons as they tried to play matchmaker), but when December hits they usually come to Rosefont Hill to visit their nans and grand-dads. It's lovely to see their lives changing as they arrive with new boyfriends/girlfriends/husbands/wives and growing families each year. Looking around the room I can see many familiar faces – Mrs Williams' grandson is still with the same girl he's been with since joining the army – a curvy brunette who always looks as though she's frowning – her grand-daughter is still single by the looks of it, but is happily chatting up Miss Brown's great-nephew, even though I know he's been with the same girl since secondary school. June Hearne (Molly's best friend for many years – there wasn't a morning that wasn't spent with the two of them gossiping on the phone together) is here with her husband John, daughter Claire and her boyfriend Steven. The two of them moved in together at the end of last year, so things are clearly serious there. Mrs Sleep possibly has the biggest family as she has four children of her own and each of them have gone on to have two or three children – all of whom are in their late teens to early thirties and no doubt about to start having families of their own. That's a difficult family to keep up with as it's so huge – but they all have the same pointy little noses, so at least that gives me some idea as to which family they belong to. And that's just a few of our regulars' families ... it's easy to see how our little hub of a community seems to expand so rapidly on special occasions.

Whilst listening to Mrs Wallis, I watch Billy walk around giving refills of mulled wine to the already tipsy customers. His warm concoction is going down a treat with everyone – something I know he'll enjoy reminding me of later on when we get home to our little house.

It amuses me watching him in this setting – not because I see him as the huge actor who won a BAFTA for his remarkable talent before opting for the quiet life for a while, but because of the reaction of others to having him there, serving them drinks in my humble little teashop. He's ridiculously charming, so it's understandable that, to a certain extent, people gush over him anyway. The local gang of teenage girls gush more than most, though. They cannot forget that he played the lead in the most obsessed-over film trilogy of the decade, *Halo*, that his poster is pinned up on their bedroom walls or that, for once, one of their heart-throbs is within their reach. Billy is oblivious to the way they still visibly melt whenever he's around – although they're far calmer now than when they first met him. If it wasn't for their shrieking and crying (yes, there were real tears involved) I'd never have found out that Billy was a famous actor – I still cringe when I think of our first few encounters. God knows what he thought of me and my unique ways – especially when I'd kicked it all off with a panic attack. I'm still not entirely sure how that progressed into us dating, but it'll be a funny story to share with our children and grandchildren one day, I'm sure.

I look through the crowds and spot Aaron and Charlotte sprawled over four chairs that they've pushed together, fast asleep – the excitement proving too much. Or perhaps they're wiped out by the dozens of cakes I saw them scoffing earlier when Colin wasn't looking, forcing them into a food-coma. Their cheeks are rosy from being outdoors for hours and then coming into the warmth of the shop (even warmer now that there are so many people squeezed inside). They're huddled close, facing each other in their scrunched-up little balls.

My heart aches when I spot Aaron's hand resting on top of his little sister's shoulder – so sweet and simple a gesture. He longs to protect her, but I know, as does he, that they've both gone through the worst they'll ever have to face in their lifetimes. Nothing could compare to the pain and confusion of having Pauline taken from them so suddenly and nothing can erase those feelings of loss and abandonment now they've felt them. It's heartbreaking that they've been exposed to so much hurt at such young ages. That their innocence has been compromised.

'Well done,' Colin whispers, breaking in on my thoughts and conversation with Mrs Wallis.

'A wonderful evening,' nods Mrs Wallis, patting my hand before tottering off in search of more wine.

'Thank you,' I smile, taking in Colin's kind eyes and round face.

'Think I might've overdone it on the mince pie

front though,' he laughs, sticking out his already slightly protruding tummy and giving it a pat.

'Good! I might've gone a little overboard on how much food I made.'

'Nonsense, Christmas is about eating as much as possible and not feeling bad for it – you've done your utmost to ensure people get into that part of the festive spirit early.'

'Including your little munchkins,' I reply, nodding to Aaron and Charlotte.

'The inhibitions of the young,' he sighs. 'How I'd love to just grab a chair and do the same myself. At what age did it become unacceptable to do so?'

His face gives a look of utter love as he takes in the adorable sight before him.

'Right, missy,' he booms in my direction, tearing his eyes away from his offspring and striding behind the counter. 'Time for you to grab a glass of Billy's finest and join in the fun.'

I try to protest but Colin doesn't listen. Instead, he picks up a clean glass, fills it with wine and places it in my hand before pulling me from my safe spot behind the counter and into the throng of the party.

'Go and enjoy the fruits of your labour . . . and if you could bring me another mince pie while you're at it I wouldn't complain,' he chuckles.

3.

I'm exhausted as I crawl into bed several hours later – never have I talked to so many people in one night. Molly was always so talkative that I didn't really need to socialize too much (something I was thankful for when she was around), and whenever Billy and I used to go out the emphasis was always on him – people didn't really bother with me, they wanted to talk to the famous one, not the ordinary girl from the teashop.

Usually I'd shy away from having conversations with people, but being in the safety of the shop, the place I love dearly and where I feel the most secure, I revelled in talking to the rowdy rabble. I'd even go as far as to say that I thoroughly enjoyed catching up with people I hadn't seen for a while. I could totally understand why Molly loved being the hostess so much – it was wonderful looking around and seeing everyone having a brilliant evening thanks to my time and effort.

Just as I'm about to let my body sink into the mattress for a well-deserved sleep, I decide to go on to the shop's Twitter account and see if anyone's tweeted. I used to hate the world of social media but the teenage customers talked me in to having one for the shop – and I'm glad they did. It's fun. I'm now forever posting photos of whatever goodies and treats I've made that day, or getting ideas from other little teashops I follow on there – plus, it's always lovely to hear from happy customers. Retweeting those messages and spreading their little nuggets of praise for all to see is so satisfying.

I grab my laptop from my bedside table, switch it on and try not to shut my eyes as the screen comes alive and the machine powers up with its loud pinging sound.

As I'm waiting for the page to load, a notification pops up on the top right of the screen to tell me I have a new email from an address I don't recognize – which usually means it's one of three things: someone who's visited the shop and wants to share their views (99.9 per cent of the time it's positive – I'll never bore of those emails); a fan asking if Billy could send them a signed photo (you have to admire their loyalty to him even though he's on a 'gap year'); or spam mail (it's shocking how much of that I get – I'm really not looking to increase the size of my willy, but thanks for the offer).

A quick glance at this email, though, stops me in my tracks and forces me to read it more thoroughly.

TO: SophieMay234@hotmail.com
FROM: proposingonthehill@yahoo.co.uk
SUBJECT: Important – your help is required for a special question

Dear Sophie,

Firstly, congratulations on arranging such a spectacular evening for us lucky lot in Rosefont Hill. Gathering around for carols is always such a special event – but having somewhere warm for us all to relax afterwards as we catch up with one another is terrific. Of course, it helps that there are delicious cakes for us to nibble on and something hot to drink!

While I was in your teashop tonight I was struck by the majestic quality it holds – it's far more than a twee little village shop. The place has a soul of its own, relaxing its visitors in its warm heart. You should be immensely pleased with what you've done with it since taking over.

My partner is a huge fan of you and your beautiful shop – she's always told me of her love for the place (she'd be in there every second of the day if it weren't for her job and other commitments), but tonight that love really came alive for me too.

My partner is the most giving, kind and thoughtful person I have ever met. I realize how lucky I am to have her in my life and how I'd do anything to keep her happy and free from worry. Life is too short not to act on such feelings.

I'd love to propose to this wonderful lady on Christmas Eve, and, if it isn't too much trouble, I'd love to do so in your beautiful teashop. I know you'll probably be wrapping things up for Christmas and looking forward to closing the shop for a while, but I'd be eternally grateful if you could help me secure my lifelong friend and the woman I want to grow old with.

I've added a separate document of the details I'd love to have included – but know your romantic little den is the perfect spot for such a big question.

The village is small, and people talk, so I hope you don't mind me keeping my identity from you . . . Hopefully, if you agree, I'll be able to thank you on the night – especially if she says yes. Fingers crossed.

Many thanks,

The Proposer
x

I stare at my computer agog, my mouth wide open in a goofy expression. I'm pretty sure I've stopped breathing.

'What?' Billy quizzes, his eyebrows knitted into an intrigued frown as he studies my face with amusement.

'Look at this!' I squeal, shoving my laptop in his face.

His eyes squint at the bright light of the screen, one of them remaining shut as he scrolls through the email. 'Whoa . . .' he says slowly with a tired smile.

'I know!'

'Who do you think it is?'

'I've no idea . . . It's not you, is it?' As soon as the question flies from my mouth I feel embarrassed. It wasn't even a properly developed thought. In fact, I don't even think I'd processed the thought at all before saying it out loud.

'Good to know you'd have rumbled my plan straightaway if it was!' he winks in a cheekily reassuring manner, letting me know that my unfiltered thoughts haven't fazed him in the slightest – he knows me and my funny mannerisms and still loves me, thankfully.

'Was anyone acting strangely tonight?' I ask.

'I don't think so . . .'

'Did you notice anyone looking gooey-eyed at their girlfriends?'

'They all were – it's Christmas. It's already romantic! Plus there was so much mistletoe; everyone had their eyes peeled to see when they could pucker up. I had to dodge my way around them all night.'

'Oh,' I gasp, realizing my error. It's not just the food I got carried away with, the décor might've been a tad on the extravagant side too, with garlands on the counter, festive wreaths on the tables with candles in their centre, fairy-lights draped around the windows and doors, and mistletoe hanging from every possible location. In my defence, I only ordered a tenner's worth from the florist – I had no idea how much that would get me and was surprised when so much arrived. I didn't want any of it to go to waste, so sprinkled the kiss-inducing sprigs everywhere. I hadn't even thought of it being an opportunity for Billy's fans to seize a chance for a good smacker. 'Sorry,' I smile sheepishly.

'Oh, don't worry . . . only Mrs Sleep managed to get her wicked way with me. She acted all innocent too – asked me to help her with her coat and then, BOOM! With a girlish laugh she suddenly realized there was mistletoe above us. She might be elderly, but she's still a little minx.'

'Oh, I'm sure.'

'And in front of her grandchildren too – the woman has no shame.'

'They probably encouraged her,' I laugh, thinking about my sweet customer who's always managed to hold a special place in my heart. I've often referred to her as my favourite (between the two of us), and that's largely down to her childlike smile and naughty glint in her eye. Even though she's in her mid-eighties, she's still out every day walking up and down the High Street and chatting to anyone who gives her the slightest eye contact. She's an inspirational little thing.

'I wonder who it is?' Billy ponders, pouting out his lips as he looks back over the email in front of us.

'Hmmm . . . I guess we'll know soon enough, although I'll see if I can piece together any clues when we email a bit more. Maybe I can get him to slip up.'

'It might not be a guy.'

'Huh?'

'Could be a woman,' he says, matter-of-factly.

'But they talk about proposing to their girlfriend.'

'Yeah . . .' Billy says slowly, raising an eyebrow at me.

'A lesbian couple?' I ask, finally catching on to what he's suggesting. Although not at all convinced that he's right, I find myself mentally going through all the females that came along last night. 'Now that would be exciting for Rosefont!'

'Well, just remember it was me who cracked the case.'

'All right, Sherlock,' I smile, before rolling my eyes.

4.

I wake the next morning to find that Billy is already out of bed and absent from my childhood bedroom – pink and girly, with a wall lined with photo frames. They used to be filled with just photos of me, my mum and dad, but a few more have been added recently. Some from my and Billy's happier times in London, one from the day I reopened Molly's, one of Molly and me on her birthday one year when we'd invited all our regulars in for a cake-fest of an afternoon (she's got cream on her nose and is pulling the funniest expression while I'm cracking up with laughter – there are even tears in my eyes) and one of Charlotte, Aaron, Colin, Billy and Mum – taken by me on a trip to feed the ducks. A wall of memories – although now I've started adding to it, I fear I'll never stop. Every morning I look at this wall and smile – it's my own little highly addictive collection of happiness.

It's very much MY room – poor Billy hasn't really had much of a say in its décor. When he turned up one day with his suitcases in the boot of the car, Mum and I couldn't refuse him entry into our humble home. Well, it's not that we couldn't – we just had no desire to. Since then, time has flown by, leaving us little time to think about our future plans. Plus, it's so easy for us both being at home that we haven't given our living arrangements much thought at all. It's quite nice having him live with us in the house I grew up in. After all, it's a place that holds a whole heap of memories for me – some good, some bad – but all have played a huge part in who I am today. Billy's brought with him a load of new energy, charm and charisma – reviving our tired little home and bringing it back to life in a whole new chapter.

When I eventually walk down the stairs a little later, Billy and Mum are already sitting at the kitchen counter talking animatedly. Mum is wide-eyed with excitement as she listens to something Billy is saying.

'Let me hazard a guess at what you two are talking about,' I tease, pulling out a seat and sitting next to Billy.

'Oh, Sophie, isn't it lovely?' Mum beams, totally side-stepping my sarcasm as she pours me a cup of tea from the pot and places it in front of me.

'Very romantic,' I agree, pouring in a splash of milk before taking a gulp. 'Now I've just got to make the whole thing perfect so that I don't disappoint the proposer . . . or the one being asked. Imagine if I totally ruin it!'

'You won't. You'll do a wonderful job, love,' Mum encourages.

'Thanks, Mum,' I smile.

'Nervous?' Billy asks with a grin, already knowing the turmoil that'll be making its way around my head.

'Of course,' I puff, feeling my cheeks redden slightly at the mere thought of the task ahead. It's a massive flipping deal. I'll be playing a role in the life-changing event of two people and I haven't the foggiest who they are. It's crazy.

'Have they emailed back?' Billy asks.

Once we'd stopped speculating over the identity of The Proposer last night, and became calmer about the whole thing, we wrote a reply confirming that we'd love to help – although I did include a few giddy lines of excitement. I couldn't help myself.

'Only a short one saying thanks and checking that I'd got the attached details of what he's after,' I say, gesturing to the piece of paper in my hand that I'd just got from the printer.

'Or she,' Billy whispers under his breath, while raising his eyebrows at me in a knowing manner.

'So, let's have a look at the specifics,' Mum says, angling the paper so that it can be read by all three of us at once. 'Oh, that all sounds so magical,' she grins as she glances over what's been requested.

Essentially I've been given a budget of £500 (but can ask for more if I think it's necessary) to transform the shop into a beautiful Christmas grotto with fairy-lights, hanging snowflakes (I'll make my own, with some paper, thread and glitter glue), candles, cakes and champagne . . . There's a woodland theme running throughout the specifics, so I think the idea is for it to look homemade, rustic and outdoorsy – it's a look I know I'll enjoy creating, and I completely understand why they've chosen Molly's as the location. It's perfect in its mismatched beauty.

'I don't think it's going to be too time-consuming either,' I think out loud, biting my bottom lip as I plan. 'The shop is already looking festive because of last night's party and the extra decorations can be made in the evenings here . . . In fact, I should probably keep everything away from the shop anyway. If any of the customers catch wind of what's going on it'll be spread around the village before we know it. There'll be a gathering of people turning up waiting to see who the mystery couple are, spoiling the whole thing. We don't want the girlfriend to suspect a thing before she walks in.'

'Good thinking,' chuckles Mum. 'I can just imagine Miss Brown and co., with their faces pressed up against the windows, trying to see what's going on.'

'Or refusing to leave on Christmas Eve,' jokes Billy, although I'm sure it's a pretty accurate description of what would happen if the news were to get out – all my wonderful elderly ladies would tie themselves to their chairs in protest, wanting the best view of the action.

'That's settled, I'll make the stuff here and will

store it and anything else I buy in a couple of boxes that we can drive over just before setting up the shop for our special guests.'

'What do you want us to do?' asks Billy.

'Just keep quiet and don't tell anyone.'

'Oh . . .' groans Mum, visibly shrinking beside me.

'What?'

'I might've told Colin.'

'What? When? You've only just found out,' I shriek in surprise at the speed of her work.

'He called this morning when we were sitting here, just after Billy had told me. Sorry love, I didn't think.'

'Don't worry. I might need Colin's help anyway. Plus, he's not exactly a gossip, is he!'

'True, true.' Mum smiles proudly at my positive assessment of Colin. 'And he said he'd love to help in any way he can.'

'Thanks, Mum.'

'I bet even the kids would love helping out with things like the snowflakes,' she suggests.

'That's a lovely idea.'

'Should I make some mulled wine?' smirks Billy.

'Funnily enough, it's been requested,' I laugh, pointing it out on the list of requirements.

'See? What did I say?' he laughs, fist pumping the air.

I roll my eyes at him.

'Are you sure you didn't write this?' I tease, raising my eyebrows at him.

Seemingly at a loss for words, Billy blushes ever so slightly before looking at Mum with a lost expression.

It's all a bit awkward, so I find myself giggling into my tea not knowing what to think.

5

The following Saturday night Colin arrives at the house
with Aaron and Charlotte, clearly having driven to the
nearest Hobbycraft before heading over. They were
each carrying a plastic bag of creative fun, filled with
pencils, felt-tips, glitter, tissue paper, sequins, tinselly
bits and pieces, as well as dried rose petals, little paper
birds and twigs to go along with the theme. Colin
blushes as he spots me looking down at the bags.

'Charlotte wouldn't leave until we had all the right
tools . . .' he shrugs.

I can't help but laugh as I look at Charlotte and see
a gleeful look on her face at getting her own way.

'It was all so pretty,' she smiles with a shrug as
Aaron silently takes the bag from her and carries it
himself – unburdening his little sister from the heavy
load and leaving her with just her tattered Minnie
Mouse.

Colin and Aaron walk past me to join Mum and
Billy in the living room (they're already busy sticking
bits and pieces together), but Charlotte holds back
and lingers – her big brown eyes looking up at me
imploringly.

'You OK?' I ask, twiddling one of the long brown
plaits that hang in front of each of her shoulders.

She nods, sheepishly.

'You sure?' It's not like her to be shy around me – maybe in the beginning she was, but not anymore.

'Am I allowed to make an angel to go on top of your Christmas tree?' she asks quietly.

'Of course!' I beam, cupping her face in my hands and giving her a hug as she giggles.

Happy with my answer, she proceeds into the room of chaos – the momentary meekness behind her.

We'd decided a night in front of the TV watching *Strictly Come Dancing* and *The X Factor* with an Indian takeaway would be the perfect conditions for working on our secret project that evening – we were quite excited to get cracking and barely spoke as we silently went about our individual tasks.

Charlotte took the most care over her angel. She is after perfection from her masterpiece, something I admire in someone so young. I watched as she delicately glued sequins and beads onto the cardboard figure Colin had assembled, her tongue sticking out in concentration as she did so.

And, two hours after starting on her creation, she presents me with the finished piece – sitting down next to me and placing her head on my shoulder as I inspect her work.

'It's gorgeous, Charlotte,' I say, leaning my head over to one side so that it touches hers.

'Do you think so?' she asks, concern in her

voice – unsure of her own success or perhaps longing to be praised some more.

'Definitely. I've never seen an angel as pretty as this one.'

'Can we give her a name?' she asks, stroking the feathers she'd patiently stuck on to her angel's wings.

'Yes, why not. What would you like to call her?'

'Pauline . . .' she almost whispers, not taking her eyes away from the angel in my hands.

It wasn't what I was expecting. A lump forms in my throat, stopping me from answering straightaway. Instead I lean over, kiss the top of her head and play with her hair fondly as I nod in response.

She looks up at me then and searches my face with a smile – such a sweet, adorable and loving smile, with only a tinge of sadness in it. Before I can smile back she clambers to her knees and puts her arms around my neck, tightly. I squeeze her back.

Sometimes words are unnecessary. Occasionally they can't match up to the mammoth feelings churning away through our veins. Every now and then, silence is best, for it speaks louder than any vowel, consonant or syllable ever could.

Breaking the moment, Charlotte gets to her feet and disappears off to the sofa to sit next to Aaron, who has already got bored of sticking and cutting and has decided to just watch *The X Factor* instead. As she hugs Minnie Mouse into herself and her eyes settle on Louis Walsh and Simon Cowell disagreeing over a contestant's talent ('But she's only sixteen, Simon!'), Charlotte looks utterly content.

My heart melts a little further.

* * *

'That was lovely,' Billy says as we are washing up the dishes once Colin, Aaron and Charlotte have left. Mum has decided to get cracking on her Christmas cards on the sofa – an arduous task that always offers such relief once completed.

Looking at my mum, and knowing her organizational skills, you'd think she'd be the sort to get them all written in September and into the post before others have even got their address books out, but it's actually a huge deal that she even does them. For years we used to skip Christmas altogether, refusing to acknowledge that the world was still turning in festive merriment when our world had been torn apart by grief. Her writing them is yet another symbol of how far she's come since those dark days of despair. It's funny to think that Christmas – a time known for its joyful togetherness – can be the loneliest time of the year for some. I'm so thankful that we're no longer lonely. That we've been found. Not by the men in our lives, either, but by ourselves.

'I miss having my family around at times like this,' Billy continues sadly as he scrapes the remains of my chicken tikka and pilau rice from my plate and into the bin.

'Oh, darling . . .'

'It's my fault; I sent them packing to LA, didn't I?'

'Not really,' I offer. 'You all just did what you thought was best.'

Once Billy's acting career had really taken off, the whole family decided to move over to America so that they could be together. Years later and they're all more than settled into their lives in the sunshine, whereas Billy decided (before meeting me) to move back to England and treat himself to the most amazing flat in central London that I've ever seen.

'Yeah . . . my mum must hate it though. She thought I'd be back over there within a few months – longing for the ease of California living, but it never happened. I stayed here.'

He rarely speaks about missing LA, his family or wanting to move back across the pond, and I wonder if a part of that is so I don't feel like I'm stopping him from being elsewhere. Now that Billy isn't tied down to acting commitments, I'm surprised he hasn't made plans to go over and see his mum, dad and siblings – instead, he seems to have been enjoying the simple life in Rosefont Hill, which, to a certain extent, I can totally understand following the mayhem of his life as a highly in-demand actor.

'Do you wish you were over there?' I ask.

'Not really. Nowhere does Christmas like England,' he smiles. 'But I just wish I could see them a bit more, you know? We used to do everything together. We were with each other all the time. And now there are only splatterings of conversations here and there. Skype can only offer you so much . . .' he exhales sadly.

'I'm sorry.'

'What for?'

'Keeping you here.'

'Oh really?' he smiles, raising his eyebrow. 'You think you're keeping me here?'

I shrug in response.

'Well, I do worry about what you'd do without my exceptional culinary skills.'

'I've taught you everything you know!' I laugh.

'True . . .'

'But I would clearly be lost without your mulled wine,' I offer.

'Exactly,' he quips before putting his arm around my waist and pulling me in for a kiss. 'I wouldn't have it any other way. I'm happy.'

'You sure?'

'There's nowhere I'd have rather been tonight than here, in this house, with your patchwork family.'

'I like that . . . patchwork family.' I repeat, mulling over the term. In my head I think of all those discarded pieces of fabric that come together to make one complete piece – something that should never work, but totally does.

'You can have it,' he winks. 'Call it an early Christmas present.'

'Argh,' I groan, his words reminding me of what's been tormenting me for weeks. 'Can we talk about this again please? What on earth can I get you?'

'Nothing.'

'Seriously, you're impossible to buy for – anything I think of buying you I realize you can afford to buy yourself better versions of.'

'Erm, are you aware of how little you pay me?' he asks, raising his eyebrows incredulously.

'I don't pay you . . .'

'Exactly,' he laughs.

'Sorry, Mr Hollywood – I'll rectify that shall I? How much would you like?' I ask, grabbing my purse from the side and jokingly scrambling together a few coins before holding them out in my hand for him to take.

'Oh, I don't think anything of monetary value would suffice . . . I'm too good,' he teases, cupping my hand so that it closes before pulling me in to his body.

'Is that so?'

'You've seen the demand for my goods,' he smirks with a playful shrug, his eyes sparkling in a cheeky manner. 'But . . .'

'Yes . . .?'

'I have some ideas about how you can keep my talents close by . . .' he whispers, his mouth brushing against my ear and causing me to giggle.

'Billy! My mum's in there.'

'I wasn't planning on getting her involved. I mean, I'm really not into that kind of thing,' he gasps in mock defiance.

'Very clever, Mr Buskin. Just don't moan when you

wake up to a lump of coal on Christmas morning,' I smirk coyly, pulling away from his clasp and continuing with the washing-up.

'Baaaaaah, humbug,' he guffaws, grabbing a tea towel, his belly laugh booming around the kitchen and filling the house with its warmth.

6.

December always seems to flash by in an instant, but it's been particularly quick this year. It's already Christmas Eve and time to close the shop for a week over the festive season – bring on some time curled up on the sofa in my PJs with lots of chocolates and plenty of sleep. We've been rushed off our feet, tirelessly working our way through the Christmas orders – dozens of homemade mince pies, Christmas cakes and puddings have been filled with boozy fruit and delivered to happy customers, each accompanied by a complimentary home-decorated red Christmas bauble to hang on their trees, on which I've handwritten in gold, glittery writing, 'Christmas won't be Christmas without any presents' – a quote from *Little Women*. I felt the need to give them all a little token of my gratitude for helping to pull me through the last six months. It would've been a lot tougher without their support and friendship.

With all our normal Christmas chores completed, and the shop announced as closed to the public at midday, it's time to move on to our secret task and unload the boxes containing all of our hard work, so that we can get the shop looking as romantic and Christmassy as possible for the big proposal.

I haven't come any closer to finding out who The Proposer is and that's because they've kept their emails short and succinct, even when I've tried to fish around for more information. Billy, Mum, Colin and I have spent so much time speculating that we're all sure to be disappointed with whoever turns up. Mum thinks that them saying they were at the Christmas gathering was a ruse to throw us all off the scent and that they have other reasons for wanting us to keep it quiet – like the pair being famous or something equally as ridiculous. Colin is adamant it's one of Mrs Sleep's brood – well, there are so many of them that the odds are in his favour there. Billy is still harping on about it being a lesbian couple, while I honestly haven't a clue.

Before Billy and I open the lid to the first box of Christmas paraphernalia, the phone rings and interrupts us. It's Mum, sounding slightly out of breath and frustrated – which isn't like her at all.

'You OK, Mum?' I ask, concerned.

'Sorry, Sophie,' she almost shouts. 'I'm with Colin and the kids. We're just getting the last few bits in for tomorrow – it's so busy here.'

'Where are you?' I ask, relieved that it's only Christmas shopping stressing her out and nothing more serious.

'The supermarket. Seriously, who decides to wait until Christmas Eve to get their Christmas dinner sorted, hey?' she says with a slight huff. 'Is there anything you need?'

'Nope, I think we're all sorted on the food front, Mum.'

'Nice and organized, I'm sure. I thought I'd only forgotten the cranberry sauce, but now we're here Colin's picking up cheese, chocolates and all sorts.'

'We have to make the most of the special offers while they're on,' I hear him protest in the background. 'They've gone into panic mode and slashed the prices on everything to get rid of it all – we'd be silly not to buy this stuff.'

'Honestly, it's not even the kids asking for it,' she sighs, probably shaking her head at him as she does so, although I can hear she's not actually annoyed. If anything she finds Colin's enthusiasm endearing and contagious. Like Billy, he injects life into an event. 'Is it OK if we pop in a little later? Before the couple arrive, obviously. Charlotte wants to put the angel on the Christmas tree herself, bless her.'

'It's just Charlotte who wants to come over, then?' I tease, knowing that they're all far too excited to stay away.

'All right, I also want to have a little nose,' she giggles, making me laugh with her.

'Of course you can. Want to come over around seven? I'm hoping everything will be done by then – if not I'll be really panicking,' I say, tapping my fingers on the top of one of the boxes that's been patiently awaiting my attention all morning but now screams in protest at the delay in its unpacking.

'Don't worry, I know you'll be fine.'

'With any luck!'

'Just let us know if you get stuck and need a hand with anything.'

'Thanks, Mum.'

'Oh my goodness – Colin's found the biggest box of Quality Street I've ever seen. Honestly, we're all going to be ten stone heavier by the end of the week if he gets his way.'

I can't help but laugh at the image of Colin naughtily dropping things in the trolley in the hope that Mum won't tell him off and make him take them out again.

'Ooh, June!' she suddenly calls, the abruptly loud sound causing me to jump and momentarily go deaf. 'Sophie, I've just bumped into June Hearne – I'm on the phone to Sophie,' she obviously says to June.

'Oh, how lovely,' I hear her say. 'Tell her I've had to come out for more mince pies already – Claire's Steven's already scoffed the ones I ordered from her,' she says, clearly put out by her daughter's boyfriend's huge appetite. 'He's never joined us for Christmas before – I never knew he could eat so much. Luckily they're off out somewhere tonight, but I'm starting to worry I'll run out of food tomorrow now.'

'Oh really? Well, you can always come to ours – Colin's buying enough to see us through to next Christmas –'

'Mum,' I call through the giggles that follow, trying to get her attention once more.

'Yes, dear?' she eventually answers.

'I've got to get started here – but I'll see you around seven.'

'OK, love. Don't forget – just give us a buzz if you need us.'

'Will do, Mum. Send my love to June,' I say before hanging up.

* * *

Donned in fluffy red Christmas hats to complete the festive look (Billy's idea – he whipped them out of his bag as soon as I got off the phone to Mum), the hours whizz by in a blur as we turn on the Christmas tunes and sing along to Frank Sinatra, Judy Garland, Michael Bublé and many more. I can't help but feel like one of Santa's little helpers as we cheerily decorate the Christmas tree, sprinkle fake snow all around us and crack on with our list of tasks. Every time I look at Billy I can't help but smile; more than ever my little shop exuberates love and romance, making me excited for our Christmas in Rosefont Hill, and our future together. I'm overcome with a feeling of completeness.

By 6:55pm we're done. Well, I'm mostly done – being the perfectionist that I am means that I can always find something to faff over. Is a job ever really finished? Is it? Not in my world.

'This looks incredible!' beams Billy as he looks around at our handiwork, placing his hand on the small of my back and gently stroking it up and down.

I stop playing with the plate of Christmas-themed

cupcakes (I was checking to see if the white chocolate snowflakes were all sitting at the same angle) and join him in looking around. It's beautiful. Garlands of fresh fir, roses, pinecones and mistletoe line the counter and sit on the weathered-looking white cabinet that usually holds gifts for people to buy and books for them to pick up and read whilst in the shop.

We don't usually have a Christmas tree in here as there's not much room for one, but at The Proposer's insistence we managed to buy a plump real one for the occasion. It's completely covered in dancing fairy-lights, and hanging from its branches are homemade wooden hearts with festive or romantic words painted onto them – Noël, love, peace, happiness, together, family . . . there's even a 'Santa'. There are also several pinecones that we'd collected from our garden and managed to turn into woodland creatures by creatively adding some further bits of wood on to them. That was actually Aaron's idea as he'd seen something on *Art Attack* and thought it might be fun. The squirrels are a little questionable, but the owls look fantastic! We've also sewn stars, Christmas trees and some more hearts (you can never have too many hearts when there's about to be a proposal) using red and green felt – it looks absolutely stunning, especially with the added magic of the lights flashing around it all.

It was impossible to put the tree in a corner as it's so big, but thankfully it doesn't take up too much of the limited floor space – instead it just stands proudly in the room, demanding our festive attention. We've cleared away a few of the tables to make space for it, but were told not to worry too much about moving out furniture. I suggested clearing all of them away and just keeping one small table and two chairs for the couple to romantically sit at, but The Proposer thought it might take away the heart of the shop (apparently the clutter is part of our charm), so most of it stayed. Instead, I've decorated them with small festive posies – red poinsettia leaves, mistletoe (yes, more of it – it's another necessity) and holly sit in a ring around chunky cream church candles, which are just waiting to be lit a little closer to the couple's arrival. I figure we'll do that at the same time we put all the fairy-lights on. In fact, the Christmas tree isn't the only place those magical little sparkling lights have been hung – we've also popped more around the cabinet so that they're draped over books and on hooks on the walls. Billy suggested having one wall covered in lights to give it a waterfall effect, but I had to put my foot down there – it would've been too much with the huge tree and all the candles that are not only on the tables, but lining the empty spots on the counter and around the edges of the room too. The place would've lit up like Times Square, rather than appearing dimly lit and atmospheric, which is what's been requested.

'Wow!' I hear Aaron proclaim as he, Charlotte, Mum and Colin walk through the door.

Charlotte's face lights up as she takes in the

room – her eyes dancing around, trying their best to take in every detail. Colin gives me a chuffed little wink and a nod of the head, clearly approving, while Mum starts crying.

'It's just so magical!' she laughs at herself, wiping her eyes.

Colin grabs her hand.

'OK, Charlotte,' I say, gesturing to the angel in her hands. 'You ready?'

After a quick glance at Colin, she looks down at the delicately feathered object and nods, before making her way towards Billy, who is waiting by the ladder at the base of the tree. Placing her spare hand in his, she slowly makes her way up the ladder, being sure to bring both feet together on each step. When she is high enough to reach the top, she stops and gives the angel in her hands a look of utter love. Bringing it to her lips, she gently kisses its head, closing her eyes tightly as she does so. We all watch as Billy places his hands around her waist to support her as she leans into the tree and slowly places the final touch to it.

My face tingles as I fight off the urge to react. I decided not to tell anyone about the angel taking on Pauline's name. I felt as though it was something to be kept between the two of us. Not that I thought Mum wouldn't understand or that she'd be put out by Pauline's presence – not at all. It just felt like something for me and Charlotte to share and keep between ourselves.

The wonderful thing about Colin is that he's always worked hard to keep Pauline's memory alive. He's forever talking about her and letting the children find new ways to express their feelings about her. It's a total contrast to how my mum and I reacted following my dad's sudden death. We shut ourselves off from the world and became completely closed books. We never spoke about Dad or the fact that he was taken away from us so abruptly. So unfairly. It was years later, once I'd met Billy, that we started having proper conversations about him and us as a family when I was growing up. One thing I've learnt from my own experiences with losing a parent is that communication is incredibly important.

Colin's doing a wonderful job with his children's loss – it's fascinating to watch. Charlotte's idea behind her angel isn't morbid, sad, shocking or uncomfortable – it's simply a way of her honouring her mum's memory. Of making her a part of her present and her future, rather than her being left in the past and something she can't talk about. It's beautiful.

Mum walks over to me and squeezes my arm. I can tell she's about to leave it there, but the emotion of the season gets the better of her again and she decides to pull me in for a hug instead. We rarely hug. Rarely show each other any form of physical comfort. It's an amazing feeling to be hugged by my mum.

'What's the time?' I ask, breaking away from our embrace – suddenly worrying that we're running behind schedule and that the couple are due to arrive any second. I wasn't expecting things to get so emotional.

'Seven-twenty,' says Colin, looking at his watch.

'You lot better go!' I start, still gripping on to Mum's hand, not really wanting to shoo them out so suddenly.

'Can we see what it all looks like without the main lights on first, love?' asks Mum.

'I don't know if we've got time now, Mum – they're going to be here in, like, ten minutes . . .'

'Oh, please!' begs Aaron. It's the first thing he's said since his initial reaction when he walked into the shop twenty minutes ago and I simply can't refuse.

'Right, Billy – pass me those matches. Let's light these candles first. It's probably good to see what it all looks like before they arrive anyway . . .' I mutter nervously, suddenly attacked by a swarm of butterflies in my tummy.

Charlotte and Aaron stand to one side as us four adults rattle around lighting candles, moving the ice bucket of champagne on to one of the tables, and general faffing to make sure everything's as it should be.

'Right, all done?' I ask, lighting the last of the candles.

'Wait!' calls Billy, walking over to the stereo. 'Can't forget the music!'

Bing Crosby's 'I'll Be Home for Christmas' starts playing and I breathe a sigh of relief that one of the requested specifics hasn't been forgotten.

'Ready now?' I ask again.

'I think so,' nods Billy, squinting as he looks around the room to check.

'Perfect, I'll get the lights,' I squeak, making my way over to the switch on the wall. 'Three, two, one!' I count down, before flicking the switch and turning the shop's overhead lights off.

There's a gasp, followed by silence.

The room has suddenly come alive with romance.

It's not the majestic lights working their magic.

It's not the Christmas tree shining in its festive joy.

It's not the handmade bits and bobs hanging from the tree or adorning every surface, nook and cranny of the shop.

It's not Bing's delectable tones crooning away.

It's the sight of Colin.

In front of my mum.

On one knee.

With Aaron and Charlotte grinning behind him, clearly in on the secret – those cheeky little monkeys.

'Jane,' he begins, pursing his lips to still his mounting nerves before taking a deep breath.

Mum looks at me in utter shock, her eyes widening as they search mine for something, anything.

A smile that I can't control spreads across my face. Big. Happy. Goofy.

She exhales and turns back to Colin who's managed to compose himself.

'I didn't know I was ready to find someone to share

my life with again until I met you. Our broken hearts bumped into each other, and from that moment I've wanted to do anything in my power to patch up your heartache and give you the love you deserve. I'm not perfect – I'm short, grey and I eat far too much, especially at Christmas – but I can offer you kindness, friendship . . . and these two little rascals,' he laughs, tilting his head towards Charlotte and Aaron behind him, who are standing hand in hand along with Minnie Mouse.

Mum's eyes are filled with tears as her shoulders come up in laughter.

'Please, Jane. Will you be my wife? Will you marry me?'

'Oh, Colin . . . Of course I will!'

Finally my tears start flowing.

Tears of complete and utter joy.

As we all sit there hearing about Colin's sneaky behaviour whilst enjoying the food I'd made and Billy's mulled wine, I find myself thinking of the angel on top of the Christmas tree and picture Pauline watching over us. I hope she's perched on a cloud somewhere in the company of Molly and Dad.

It comforts me to think of them with us on this special occasion. As Colin has proven with his children, the world is a much happier place when you keep their memories alive – rather than shutting them away into the big dark hole of the past. Now I make a conscious effort not to shy away from the absence of the loved ones we've lost. Instead, I choose to think of them and honour them, to include them, to make them a part of our family's future. They're with us and I feel the love bouncing around the festive room.

Our little family might be unconventional, with bits missing or broken, but in this moment I feel nothing but pride, love and happiness. I feel complete.

7.

'OK, now, I didn't know what to get you,' I say, picking up Billy's gift from under the tree and walking over to him.

'You didn't have to get me anything . . .'

'But I wanted to,' I say, raising my eyebrows as I place a huge box on the floor in front of him. The kids have already opened all of their gifts and have run off excitedly to have a go on their new bikes in the garden. Mum and Colin have gone to watch, although they've spent the majority of the morning in a bubble for two. It's adorable to see them both looking so in love and engrossed with their affection for one another.

'Whoa, not as heavy as it looks,' he says, picking up the almost empty box.

'I wanted to keep you guessing,' I admit. 'I'm surprised you haven't been down here shaking it trying to guess.'

'How do you know I haven't?' he grins before tearing into the glittery red wrapping, opening the box and taking out its contents. 'An envelope . . .' he vocalizes, looking puzzled as he turns it from one side to the other repeatedly as if its exterior will give him a clue.

I can't help but giggle as I watch him finally open it and take out the airline tickets.

'What? We're going to LA?!' he proclaims after reading their destination.

'Yep. In two days, for two whole weeks.'

'But, what about the shop?'

'It's all sorted. Mum's due some holiday time from the library and Colin's offered to help out too.' I can't help but grin at his expression.

'We'll be having New Year in LA?'

'With your family,' I nod.

'Do they know?'

'Of course they do,' I laugh. 'I had to check they weren't going off on holiday or anything. I would've booked a hotel, but your Mum has insisted we stay with them.'

'I bet she has. I can't believe she hasn't slipped up – she must be so excited.'

'She sounded it.'

'Thank you so much, Sophie!' he says, getting up off the floor and scooping me into his arms so that my feet are up off the ground. 'I can't believe you're going to meet my family, though . . . You don't know what you're letting yourself in for there.'

'They've all sounded lovely on the phone,' I shrug – although secretly I'm pretty nervous about meeting the Buskin clan. I've never been particularly good with new people – especially important people like potential in-laws (here's hoping . . . one day).

'That's what they want you to think,' he laughs.

'Just wait until they get their claws into you – Mum will have you agreeing to all sorts!'

I'm thrilled that he's visibly excited about seeing his family. Although it makes me question more than ever why he hadn't planned the trip himself – even if I weren't able to go with him because of the shop. He's clearly missed them more than he's let on.

'Now it's time for yours,' Billy winks, walking over to the tree and bringing back a fairly big present – wrapped in brown paper, but with a big festive red bow placed on the top. The tag on the present reads, 'Christmas . . . a time for remembering, cherishing and uniting. Life presents us with a series of patches, and from those little patches great things are made. Merry Christmas. Billy. Xx.'

Opening it, I'm greeted by a rainbow of colours. Dozens of different fabrics, of various textures, shapes and sizes, have been sewn together to create one ginormous, warm and cosy quilt.

A beautiful patchwork quilt, to match my beautiful patchwork family.

MERRY CHRISTMAS!

Giovanna's Top Tips for a Very Merry Christmas

I love Christmas and I'm not ashamed to admit that we put our Christmas tree up on the earliest possible date – one year it was even up in November! It's the one time of year when you can curl up on the sofa and stuff your face full of chocolate without anyone thinking badly of you – surely that alone is a reason to rejoice?

If you don't find it quite so easy to slip into the spirit of the season, here are a few Christmassy tips from me to you:

1. Write all your Christmas cards. You're bound to feel extra Christmassy after you've written 'Merry Christmas' a hundred times!

2. Grab yourself a big bowl and overload it with chocolates – Ferrero Rocher, Cadbury's Roses, Quality Street, Lindt Balls . . . all of the greats! Put them on the coffee table in your lounge and *slowly* make your way through them (you don't want to peak too early). If other people come over, you can enjoy a group appreciation of chocolate . . . or you can just hide them all. Sharing is caring, but not when it comes to Ferrero Rocher!

3. Get your friends over and play Balderdash. If you've never heard of it before, go out and invest – it's the ultimate Christmas board game!

4. Make mince pies and eat a few while they're still hot. Be careful not to burn your mouth though – rookie mistake.

5. Give those neighbours whom you never talk to a festive treat – nothing like the aforementioned homemade mince pies to bring the community together!

6. Whack on the Christmas tunes and enjoy singing 'All I want for Christmas is yoooooooooou!' at the top of your lungs.

7. Go to a Christmas tree farm. I didn't know these actually existed until a few years ago, but I now love the idea of going along and picking our tree out . . . as long as some cute little animals haven't already bagsied it for their home, of course!!

8. Go see Santa! Yep, go sit on the old guy's knee and spiel off all the things you want this year.

9. Get the Argos catalogue out. When I was a kid we used to turn down the corners of our favourite pages in the hope that we'd be given them all for Christmas . . . talk about subtle hints!

10. Hire a snow machine. OK, this might be slightly extravagant – perhaps just learn a tribal snow dance and perform that around your living room instead.

Discover *Billy and Me*, Giovanna Fletcher's
gorgeously romantic debut novel!

What would you do if you fell in love
with both your best friends?

Giovanna Fletcher

You're
The One
that I want